MADELINE

story & pictures by
Ludwig Bemelmans

THE VIKING PRESS · NEW YORK

Viking Seafarer edition issued in 1969 by The Viking Press, Inc.
625 Madison Avenue, New York, N.Y. 10022

Distributed in Canada by
The Macmillan Company of Canada Limited

Library of Congress catalog card number: 39–21791

Pic Bk

SBN 670–05023–7

2   3   4   5   6   75   74   73   72   71

PRINTED IN U.S.A.

In an old house in Paris

that was covered with vines

lived twelve little girls in two straight lines.

In two straight lines they broke their bread

and brushed their teeth

and went to bed.

They smiled at the good

and frowned at the bad

and sometimes they were very sad.

They left the house

at half past nine

in two straight lines

in rain

or shine—

the smallest one was Madeline.

She was not afraid of mice —

she loved winter, snow, and ice.

To the tiger in the zoo

Madeline just said, "Pooh-pooh,"

and nobody knew so well

how to frighten Miss Clavel.

In the middle of one night
Miss Clavel turned on her light
and said, "Something is not right!"

Little Madeline sat in bed,

cried and cried—her eyes were red.

And soon after Dr. Cohn

came, he rushed out to the phone,

and he dialed: DANton-ten-six —

"Nurse," he said, "it's an appendix!"

Everybody had to cry—

not a single eye was dry.

Madeline was in his arm

in a blanket safe and warm.

In a car with a red light

they drove out into the night.

Madeline woke up two hours
later, in a room with flowers.

Madeline soon ate and drank.

On her bed there was a crank,

and a crack on the ceiling had the habit
of sometimes looking like a rabbit.

Outside were birds, trees, and sky —
and so ten days passed quickly by.

One nice morning Miss Clavel said,

"Isn't this a fine—

day to visit

Madeline."

VISITORS FROM TWO TO FOUR

read a sign outside her door.

Tiptoeing with solemn face,

with some flowers and a vase,

in they walked and then said, "Ahhh,"
when they saw the toys and candy
and the dollhouse from Papa.

But the biggest surprise by far—

on her stomach

was a scar!

"Good-bye," they said, "we'll come again,"

and the little girls left in the rain.

They went home and broke their bread

brushed their teeth

and went to bed.

In the middle of the night
Miss Clavel turned on the light
and said, "Something is not right!"

And afraid of a disaster

Miss Clavel ran fast

and faster,

and she said, "Please children do —

tell me what is troubling you?"

And all the little girls cried, "Boohoo,
we want to have our appendix out, too!"

"Good night, little girls!

Thank the Lord you are well!

And now go to sleep!"

said Miss Clavel.

And she turned out the light —

and closed the door —

and that's all there is —

there isn't any more.